W9-CLR-559

DISCARD

SUPERSUITS

SUPERSUITS

by Vicki Cobb

Illustrated by Peter Lippman

J. B. LIPPINCOTT COMPANY
Philadelphia and New York

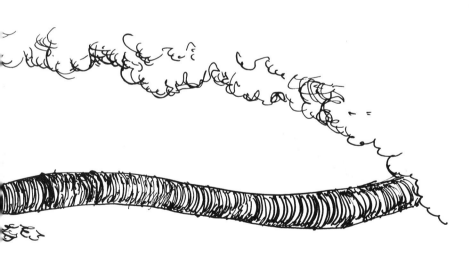

The author gratefully acknowledges permission to reprint the following poems:

"Fire" by Wallace Irwin from *Shrieks at Midnight* by Sara and John Brewton. Copyright © 1969 by Sara and John Brewton, with permission of Thomas Y. Crowell Company, Inc., publisher.

"Cold Fact" by Dick Emmons. Reprinted with permission from *The Saturday Evening Post* © 1956 The Curtis Publishing Company.

"Sea Shanty" from *Collected Poems* by Clifford Dyment. Reprinted by permission of J. M. Dent & Sons, Ltd., publishers.

"How to Tell the Top of a Hill" from *The Reason for the Pelican* by John Ciardi. Copyright © 1959 by John Ciardi. Reprinted by permission of J. B. Lippincott Company.

U.S. Library of Congress Cataloging in Publication Data

Cobb, Vicki.
    Supersuits.

    SUMMARY: Describes severe environmental conditions that require special clothing for survival—conditions involving freezing cold, fire, underwater work, and thin or non-existent air.
    1. Clothing, Protective—Juvenile literature. 2. Cold—Physiological effects—Juvenile literature. 3. Heat—Physiological effects—Juvenile literature. 4. High pressure (Technology)—Physiological effects—Juvenile literature. [1. Clothing, Protective. 2. Man—Influence of environment] I. Lippman, Peter J., illus. II. Title.
    TT649.C62   508.3′028   74-19083
    ISBN-0-397-31559-7   ISBN-0-397-31609-7 (pbk.)

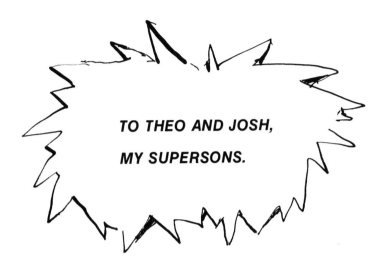

TO THEO AND JOSH,
MY SUPERSONS.

The author expresses gratitude and appreciation to Carl Proujan for sharing his South Pole experiences; to William Cole for aiding in the search for mood-setting poetry; to Josephine Hendin for constructive comments; to the United States Air Force, Navy, and NASA for providing information on the latest fashions for hostile environments; and to New York's Bravest—the Fire Department—for conveying their view of life, death, and inferno.

Contents

SUPERSUITS

COLD FACT

By the time he's suited
And scarved and booted
And mittened and capped
And zipped and snapped
And tucked and belted,
The snow has melted.

Dick Emmons

1 *Going Where It's Cold*

There are some natives of Australia who are famous for sleeping completely naked on frozen ground. It's no special trick for them because they've been doing it all their lives, and their bodies have become used to the cold. But if you tried to do as they do, you would spend a sleepless and miserable night—a night that could be extremely dangerous to your health.

That's because you are used to wearing clothing. Clothing prevents body heat from escaping into the air. It keeps the air next to your body at a comfortable and safe temperature. Clothing has also made it possible for the human race, which is nearly hairless, to live in parts of the world that can get much colder than Australia. Heavy clothing is protection against cold winter weather.

Some parts of the world are so cold that most people wouldn't want to settle there, even if they had the proper clothing. But for some people, the coldest parts of earth are an invitation to adventure and new knowledge. They know that bitter cold can mean discomfort, danger, and even death. Yet they rise to its challenge and prove that people can survive where cold is the greatest enemy.

THE EARTH'S DEEP FREEZE

Your winter clothes won't keep you warm very long at the coldest place on earth—Antarctica, site of the South Pole. It's so cold there that it's hard to tell whether today is colder or warmer than yesterday. In fact, we wouldn't know what day was the coldest without an instrument to measure air temperature.

Weather stations in most places on earth usually measure air temperatures with mercury thermometers. Mercury is a metal that is liquid at ordinary temperatures. A mercury thermometer is a hollow glass tube that has a bulb filled with mercury at one end. When the temperature of the air around the bulb gets warmer, the mercury grows larger. It moves up the tube, appearing as a silvery line. When surrounding air gets cooler, the mercury shrinks, making a shorter line. Marks along the length of the tube, called *degrees,** show just how long the mercury line is. And this length is read as the temperature.

Mercury thermometers can measure temperature as long as the mercury is liquid. But at about 38°F below zero, mercury freezes. Solid mercury is not able to grow and shrink to show changes in temperature. In Antarctica, the average temperature is about 57°F below zero—about 19° lower than the freezing point of mercury. Thermometers here contain a kind of alcohol instead of mercury. Alcohol, which is also used as antifreeze in car radiators, remains a liquid at these low temperatures.

* There are two kinds of thermometers, Fahrenheit and Celsius. A Fahrenheit degree (° F) is smaller than a Celsius degree (° C). That is, the distance between degree lines on thermometers the same length is shorter on a Fahrenheit thermometer.

An alcohol thermometer was used to measure the lowest temperature ever found anywhere on earth—127°F below zero. It was recorded about one thousand miles from the South Pole in the heart of Antarctica. At such low temperatures rubber breaks like glass, and a steel bar can snap in two. Fuel for running engines is as thick as molasses. Special machinery is used here for transportation and outdoor work.

Antarctica is famous for its winds as well as its cold. The usual gust of wind there blows at about fifty miles an hour. That's strong enough to lift off the tops of some chimneys. Often there are gusts of hurricane strength—more than seventy-five miles an hour. Buildings in Antarctica are built close to the ground to prevent damage by high winds.

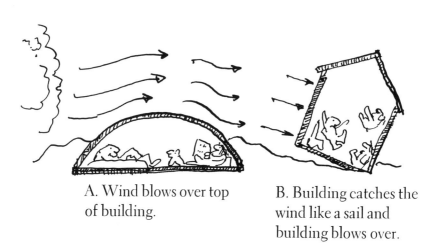

A. Wind blows over top of building.

B. Building catches the wind like a sail and building blows over.

Winds also make low temperatures feel even lower. Scientists call this "wind chill." If you add the usual wind chill to the usual cold temperatures, it's as if you were in a temperature of about 105°F below zero on an average day in Antarctica. If you add wind chill to the lowest Antarctic temperatures it's as if you were in a temperature of about 200°F below zero. That's a lot colder than a Midwestern winter!

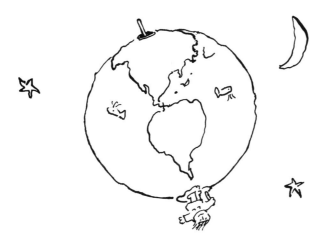

THE SOUTH POLE SCENE

At the South Pole, the bottom of the world, there are really only two seasons, a long winter and a short summer. They are not like the seasons you probably know. There are no trees to blossom and lose their leaves. And it is always cold. The "hottest" summer day here is 5°F above zero. Winter temperatures are usually 80°F to 90°F below zero.

Winter and summer at the South Pole are as different as night and day. In fact, they *are* night and day. The end of winter comes on September 21 when the sun rises. For six months the sun never sets.

People here think of November, December, and January as summer. That's the working season when, day by day, the sun gets higher in the sky until it's high enough to warm things up a bit. The nine-month winter begins as the sun gets lower. On March 21 the sun sets, bringing the heart of the Antarctic winter. For six long months there is only night at the South Pole. Bitter cold and howling winds rule the ice. It's not the time many dare make a visit.

If you visited the South Pole, you would probably come on an Antarctic summer day. It feels almost like another world here, not a part of the earth we call home. The cloudless summer sky is very blue. You are surrounded by a bright field of snow that stretches as far as you can see, like a frozen desert. The sunlight looks as it does at three in the afternoon at home. But here the height of the sun doesn't give you a clue to what time it is. It never gets any higher or lower in the sky all day. It simply moves around the sky in a circle, as bright at midnight as it is at noon.

On this day it is about 19°F below zero, about average for summer. As you look around, you see a cloud of ice crystals suddenly appear in the air and sparkle like diamonds in the sunlight.

This happens only in very cold, dry air. Air where you live has water in it. You can't see this water, because it is in the form of a gas. Extra water in air can be "squeezed out" as droplets in the form of dew or fog. Warm air can hold a great deal of water vapor before droplets form. But at Antarctic temperatures air can hold hardly any water at all. Moisture that escapes into the air from the surface of the snow is squeezed out and frozen instantly in clouds of glittering ice crystals. Moisture from your breath also crackles and freezes the instant it meets the cold, dry polar air.

Of course, a trip to the South Pole is never spoiled by rain. In fact, it hardly ever snows there. Only about two inches of snow fall every year. That's not even enough for good sledding! But wait. It never gets warm enough for snow to melt. For millions of years snow has piled up. As the weight of new snow presses on snowfalls of the past, old snow changes into ice. Today Antarctica is covered with a pile of ice, topped with snow, that is almost two miles high in many places. No wonder scientists and Navy personnel who work here call the Antarctic continent "the ice."

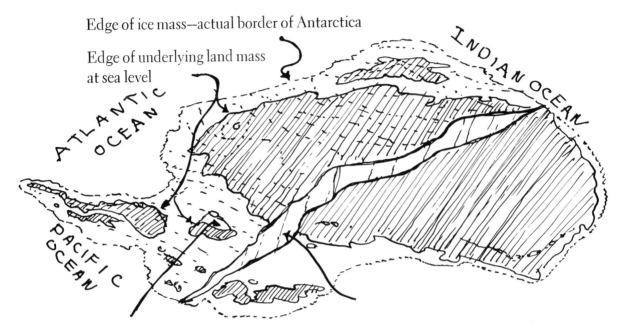

Edge of ice mass—actual border of Antarctica

Edge of underlying land mass at sea level

ATLANTIC OCEAN

PACIFIC OCEAN

INDIAN OCEAN

Vinson Massif, 16,860 feet above sea level, is a tall mountain that sticks up above the ice. If the ice were gone, it would be an island.

Ice cut through to show thickness. The thickness varies depending on the contour of the land. Roughly at this point the ice is 2½ miles thick (13,200 feet). It extends both below and above sea level.

THE CALL OF ANTARCTICA

It is not beautiful scenery that brings people to Antarctica. It is not ice crystals in the air. It is not the hotels. (There are none.) And it is certainly not the weather. People come to Antarctica to learn. Many nations have agreed to share Antarctica peacefully. Scientists come here from all over the world to unlock the mysteries of nature's deep freeze.

There are secrets in the ice. Great masses of ice, called glaciers, once covered much of the earth. Glaciers creep over land like heavy, slow-moving rivers. They drag along rocks that scratch the land like giant fingernails. They push soil around like monster bulldozers. When they melt, they leave behind hills of rocks and soil.

Most of the glaciers that once covered the earth are gone. We know of them from scars and rocks they left behind. But these scars can teach us only a small amount about the ways of glaciers, just as footprints can only teach us a little about the animals that left them. To understand how glaciers change the face of the earth, scientists want to study the real thing. Antarctica is one of the few places left on earth where they can see a glacier in action.

The glaciers of Antarctica also hold a key to earth's history. Layers of ice, laid down year after year, have a message scientists can read. They can tell scientists when the earth was warm and when it grew colder. Air from millions of years ago is trapped in the ice. Scientists drill into the glaciers for ice samples to study the past.

Under the ice, if you drill deep enough, there is land. It is the Antarctic continent, which is as large as the United States and Mexico together. Scientists have found the preserved remains of tropical plants and animals in Antarctic soil. This discovery can only mean that once, millions of years ago, Antarctica was warm. Scientists believe that somehow the Antarctic land mass drifted to the bottom of the earth from a place farther north. They know that other land masses on earth have moved and are still moving (so slowly you would never notice it). By learning more about the movement of Antarctica we add to our knowledge of the shifting positions of other parts of the earth.

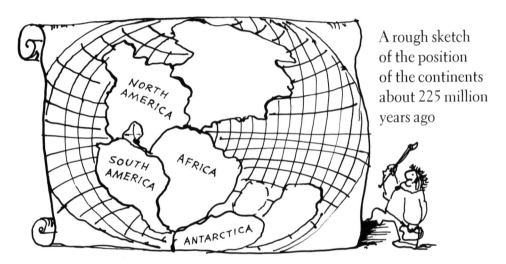

A rough sketch of the position of the continents about 225 million years ago

Scientists also come to the South Pole to study the strange lights that glow overhead during the Antarctic night. (It's a cold and lonely world for the few hardy people who "winter over" the polar night.) These "southern lights" are caused by the earth acting like a magnet on electrical particles in the air. They are clues helping us understand the earth's core and the upper edges of its blanket of air.

Even pollution is a reason for scientists to come to Antarctica. Air and water pollution from other parts of the world come here in wind and ocean currents. By measuring pollution here, scientists can see how fast it is spreading around the world.

Although Antarctica is bitterly cold and dry, it is not lifeless. Penguins and seals raise families on its rocky shores. Fish and small plants live in its icy seas. Perhaps their secrets of survival can help us survive better. It's something some scientists are looking into.

Scientists come to learn. But they need housing, heat, food, and contact with the rest of the world. So others come to provide these services. Cargo ships arrive with supplies. Planes bring visitors and supplies to inland areas. People from newspapers and magazines come to do stories about the work going on here.

But everyone who comes, from scientist to radio operator to cook, has another reason deep inside. Going to Antarctica is an adventure. It is dangerous. Many of the first voyagers to come here died. Visitors (everyone here is only a visitor) feel that they are following in the footsteps of the first brave explorers. Deep inside, everyone has a question that waits for an answer. You too may wonder, "Can I face danger and handle it well?" Antarctica is one place where an answer can be found.

DANGERS OF THE DEEP FREEZE

You have a warm body. Normal body temperature is about 98°F. If the air is warm, say 80°F, you don't feel cold even if you have nothing on. Lower the temperature by 10° and you soon begin feeling chilly. Lower it again to 60°F and you'll soon be uncomfortably cold.

The low temperatures of Antarctica can kill, no question about it. Cold air sucks heat away from warm bodies. Heat leaves quickly from exposed skin. You can also cool off slowly, through your clothing, if you spend hours outdoors. You lose heat first from your hands and feet, then from your arms and legs. Finally the temperature of the rest of your body drops.

Your hands and feet usually have a lower temperature than the rest of your body. But you'll have trouble using them as they get even colder. When the skin temperature of your hands drops to 60°F, your fingers will be so numb you won't even be able to tie your shoe.

As your body temperature drops from 98°F, it first fights against losing heat. "Goose bumps" make the layer of quiet air next to your skin thicker. Quiet air is protection, or *insulation*, that slows down heat loss. Then you begin to shiver. You know how you get warm when you exercise. Shivering is exercise you can't control. It's your body's way of producing more heat. The trouble is that shivering can't make up for heat that has already been lost. It can only slow down the loss of additional body heat.

As your temperature gets still lower, shivering becomes

more and more violent. Then, as your body reaches about 90°F, you stop shivering and your muscles get stiff. At this point, if you're like most people, you pass out. You breathe more slowly. Your heart loses its steady beat and finally stops altogether at about 75°F.

Many people have had their bodies cooled lower than this and survived. Doctors carefully control the cooling of patients during certain operations. Some people, cooled by exposure to cold weather, were discovered and warmed up before they froze. Death is certain if the human body freezes.

There are different opinions about why freezing kills people. Some think it isn't freezing that's fatal but the way living things are thawed out. Some people believe that freezing could be used to preserve people shortly after they die of natural causes. They think that scientists of the future, perhaps hundreds of years from now, will have solved all the problems of disease, death, and defrosting. Dead bodies, frozen today, could be thawed far in the future, revived, and cured of the sickness that killed them in the first place. Think of that! A time machine from the deep freeze.

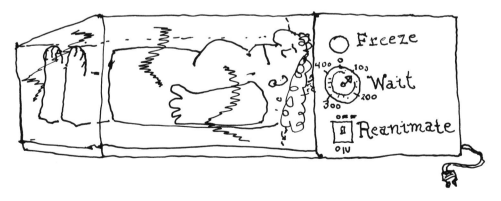

There's not much chance it will happen. It may not be the defrosting process that does the deadly damage after all. The killer may be ice crystals. When water freezes, it takes up more space. Ice crystals formed in flesh press against its delicate structure. This might cause so much damage that life can't continue after thawing. Or perhaps freezing removes water from living material. Perhaps flesh becomes permanently damaged from lack of water.

There is little danger of your whole body freezing, even in Antarctica. Most people are protected by clothing. There is a much greater danger of frostbite where exposed patches of skin freeze. The most likely place to get frostbite is the nose, which is usually left uncovered. (You have to breathe, after all.)

Frostbite can happen very quickly. At extremely low temperatures your face can freeze within thirty seconds after you step outside. In such a case you would be warned by a sharp pricking as the cold attacked. If you rushed inside and warmed up the frozen area quickly with hot water, without rubbing, there would be no permanent damage. But you might not feel this warning if frostbite came on more slowly. Cold skin gets numb and can freeze without your feeling a thing. That's why in Antarctica people are always checking each other, especially noses, for early signs of frostbite. Frostbitten skin is easily spotted. It has a yellowish white look to it.

Sunlight and glare off snow are another Antarctic danger. If your eyes get too much light from these two

24

sources, snow blindness is the unhappy result. It comes from spending six hours or more in very bright light without protecting your eyes. A few hours later you feel a pricking as if you had sand in your eyes. It gets worse until you feel as if your eyes were full of sand. Tears roll down your cheeks and even dim light hurts your eyes. Twelve hours later your eyelids are twitching. Gradually, within a few days, you recover. Snow blindness may not last forever, but it's no picnic, that's for sure.

If you had the chance to go to Antarctica, would you take it? The coldest place on earth is a land of great danger and great promise. To face its challenge you must come protected against wind, unbelievable cold, and glaring light. You need a supersuit for the deep freeze. If you turn the page you can see the latest fashion. . . .

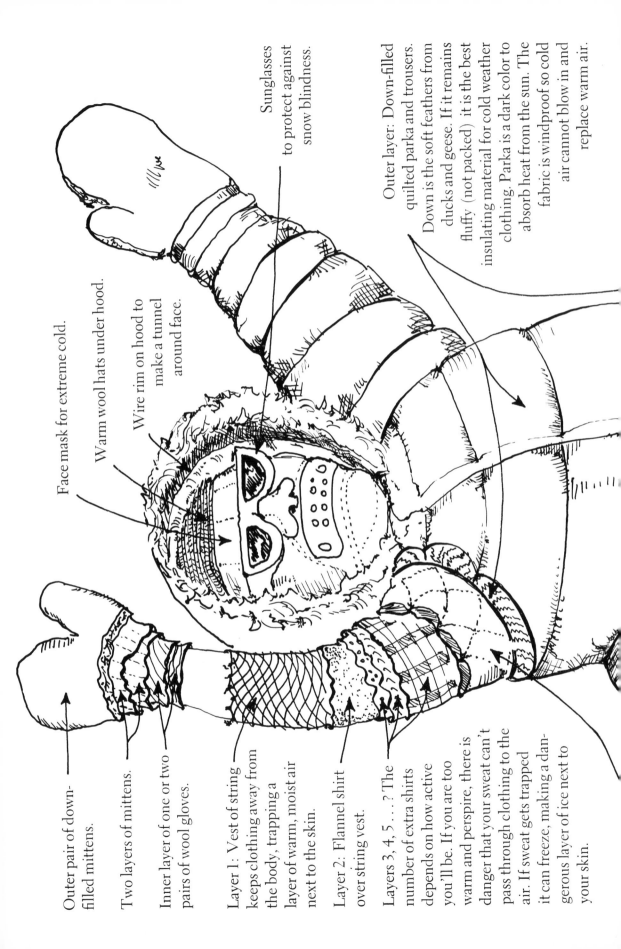

Sunglasses to protect against snow blindness.

Outer layer: Down-filled quilted parka and trousers. Down is the soft feathers from ducks and geese. If it remains fluffy (not packed) it is the best insulating material for cold weather clothing. Parka is a dark color to absorb heat from the sun. The fabric is windproof so cold air cannot blow in and replace warm air.

Face mask for extreme cold.

Warm wool hats under hood.

Wire rim on hood to make a tunnel around face.

Layer 1: Vest of string keeps clothing away from the body, trapping a layer of warm, moist air next to the skin.

Layer 2: Flannel shirt over string vest.

Layers 3, 4, 5 …? The number of extra shirts depends on how active you'll be. If you are too warm and perspire, there is danger that your sweat can't pass through clothing to the air. If sweat gets trapped it can freeze, making a dangerous layer of ice next to your skin.

Outer pair of down-filled mittens.

Two layers of mittens.

Inner layer of one or two pairs of wool gloves.

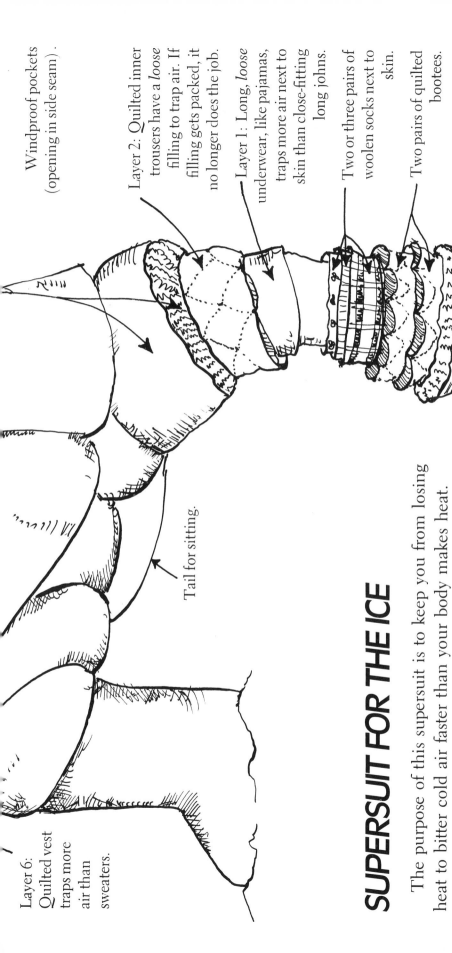

Windproof pockets (opening in side seam).

Layer 2: Quilted inner trousers have a *loose* filling to trap air. If filling gets packed, it no longer does the job.

Layer 1: Long, *loose* underwear, like pajamas, traps more air next to skin than close-fitting long johns.

Two or three pairs of woolen socks next to skin.

Two pairs of quilted bootees.

Down-filled boots with canvas covering. Footwear lets perspiration escape so ice doesn't form next to feet.

Layer 6: Quilted vest traps more air than sweaters.

Tail for sitting.

SUPERSUIT FOR THE ICE

The purpose of this supersuit is to keep you from losing heat to bitter cold air faster than your body makes heat. Insulation slows down heat loss. Quiet, trapped air is the best insulation. Air is trapped between layers of clothing, so the secret of this supersuit is many layers of trapped air insulation.

FIRE

Arthur with a lighted taper
Touched the fire to grandpa's paper.
Grandpa leaped a foot or higher,
Dropped the sheet and shouted "Fire!"
Arthur, wrapped in contemplation,
Viewed the scene of conflagration.
"This," he said, "confirms my notion—
Heat creates both light and motion."

Wallace Irwin

2 Going Where There's Fire

Your body is like a furnace. It produces heat constantly, as long as you are alive. Yet, most of the time, your body temperature stays at about 98°F. You don't keep getting warmer and warmer, because body heat is always escaping into the air.

When surrounding air is cold, heat is lost quickly. Your body responds by producing more heat. But when air temperature is near body temperature, heat doesn't escape as quickly. Then your body must work to keep you cool.

Think of how you feel on a 95°F summer day. Hot and sweaty. When perspiration evaporates into the air, it cools your skin. (The evaporation of water off your skin after a bath or shower is what makes you feel chilly.) Blood rushes to the skin, where the cooling action is. That's why you look redder than usual when you're hot. Cooled blood then moves deeper into your body, keeping body temperature down.

It's a good thing that your skin works to keep you cool. If your body temperature goes only one degree above normal, even things you know how to do well, like reading a book, will give you trouble. (Remember how bad you felt

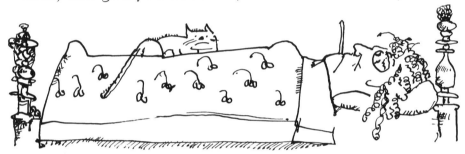

the last time you had a fever.) Your amazing skin can keep your temperature from rising even if the air is a few degrees warmer than you are.

Of course, there are limits. If air temperature gets high enough, all the sweat you can muster won't keep you cool. Slowly but surely body temperature rises if you spend too much time in air 20° to 30° warmer than you are.

Yet there are brave people, firefighters, who often spend time where temperatures are higher than 120°F. And heat is just one of the dangers they face. Not only is a raging fire unpleasant and uncomfortable, it can be a death trap in more ways than one.

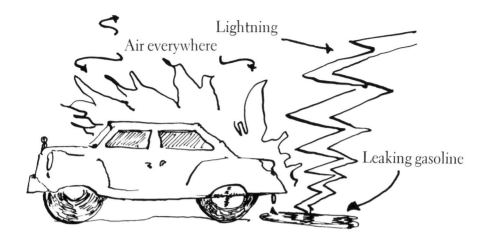

Lightning

Air everywhere

Leaking gasoline

ABOUT FIRE AND HUMAN LIFE

It takes three things to make a fire—fuel, oxygen, and a source of heat. There are countless numbers of possible fuels, including houses, forests, airplanes, garbage—and people. Air supplies oxygen. Most of the time fuel and oxygen exist together without burning. But the presence of that third ingredient—a lit cigarette, a cinder from a camp fire, a spark from a bare wire—lets nature take over.

Fires usually begin small. When there is enough fuel and oxygen, they spread. Burning continues until the fuel or oxygen is used up or until the temperature is lowered. But before a fire stops burning, it can destroy life and property.

During a fire, fuel is changed into smoke and gases. Flames are the heat and light given off by burning gases, and they are very hot indeed! Flames, smoke, gas, and heat—each has a special way of making life miserable for a person near a large fire blazing out of control.

When flames meet skin, burns are the result. Anyone caught in the middle of flames will be quickly roasted. Yet flames are not the greatest danger for professional fire-fighters.

Flames are easy to see and stay clear of. They are so unpleasant that firefighters avoid them without thinking. Luckily they can put out flames without getting too near them. Most burns firefighters get come from an unhappy surprise such as a floor collapsing or a falling cinder.

Smoke is a mixture of gases and tiny specks of unburned fuel which make smoke look gray or black. Since smoke spreads through the air, it is impossible for firefighters to get anywhere near a fire without breathing smoke. Make no mistake—when you breathe in smoke, you know it! Smoke is irritating to eyes, lungs, and windpipe.

Your body responds to protect you. Tears run down your cheeks. Tears are nature's eyewash to clear your eyes. Inside your nose and windpipe a thicker fluid, called *mucus*, forms. Mucus keeps specks of smoke from getting to the moist, tender lining of your air passages. You also cough a lot to send the nasty stuff back where it came from. All this feels pretty awful, which is a good thing. It makes you leave a smoky place (hopefully, there is a way out) before the smoke can do real damage.

More dangerous than smoke are poisonous gases that don't warn you with pain. The most common of these is carbon monoxide, which has no smell or taste to tip you off. It forms in fires that have enough oxygen to smolder

but not enough to burn with a flame. You can count on it to be around in underground fires and fires in closed spaces.

Carbon monoxide stops your body from getting oxygen. If you breathe enough of it, you die as if you were smothered. Firefighters try to make sure fires have enough oxygen so carbon monoxide doesn't form. That's why they make a hole in the roof of a burning building when they begin attacking a fire. As air reaches a fire it burns more quickly. But this makes fire fighting easier because flames now show where the fire is. And instead of carbon monoxide, there is only harmless old carbon dioxide (the gas that is the fizz in soda).

Other poisonous gases may form at a fire, depending on what's burning. Many of today's buildings contain plastics and rubber that give off an assortment of deadly fumes when they burn. When wool, leather, meat, or hair burns (as in warehouse fires), you get hydrogen sulfide, which smells like rotten eggs. Along with this you might also get irritating sulfur dioxide, one of the main gases forming air pollution. If a building has been treated with roach poison, you might get hydrogen cyanide and its lovely smell of bitter almonds. Hydrogen cyanide is the gas used in gas chambers. Usually fires produce more than one of these gases in deadly combination. Many victims of fire die of smoke poisoning, before they are touched by flames or heat.

Heat is probably the worst enemy of firefighters. It's heat that makes a fire spread. Some materials, such as paper and oily rags, burn at lower temperatures than others, such as wood. The heat of a spark is enough to start paper burning in a wastebasket. This small fire provides enough heat to light up curtains. Burning curtains set wooden window frames blazing, and before you know it a room becomes a torch that spreads fire to the rest of a house. If there is enough heat, even iron will burn.

A combination of heat and hard work makes firefighters sweat. If they keep at it for a few hours, they'll lose a great deal of water from their bodies. Loss of fluid can lead to a condition called heat exhaustion. (Collapse from heat exhaustion can also happen if you spend a day in the hot sun.) Rest and fluids are a simple cure.

Things get rougher as temperatures get higher. Heat causes burns if skin temperature reaches 111°F. Since it takes a few minutes for skin to reach this temperature, firefighters can stay in air that hot for short periods of time. Air that is 131°F will burn the skin after twenty seconds. At 158°F, skin burns in one second. If water hits a fire, the air fills with steam. Moist air causes burns at lower temperatures than dry air.

Even if the temperature doesn't get high enough to cause burns, heat can kill. If body temperature rises too much, the body's normal cooling system may fail and heatstroke results. Sometimes a person is warned by a feeling of giddiness or confusion. Other times there is no warning. The victim stops sweating, then loses consciousness. If body temperature reaches 110°F, death is almost certain. First aid for heatstroke is rapid cooling.

THE JOY OF FIRE FIGHTING

Fires can injure and kill in many dreadful ways. This is something no one has to be told. The natural reaction is to run *away* from fire. Yet firefighters do just the opposite. They choose to move at top speed to the waiting dangers. They brave heat. They breathe smoke. They take their chances with deadly gases. Why do they do it?

Some shrug and say, "It's a job." True. But there are easier and less dangerous ways to earn a living. To become a firefighter, you must take many tests. Only the best are chosen. People who get to be firefighters are smart enough and strong enough to be successful at safer jobs. Clearly, fire fighting has other things going for it.

Fire fighting means action. When the alarm sounds, you don't sit around and discuss the problem. You don't write for permission to do your thing. You move! It's all so simple. There is a fire. Your job is to help put it out. The sooner you get to it, the better.

Firefighters never know what to expect. Every fire is different. Sometimes a fire is a special challenge. A fire in a skyscraper must be attacked differently from a fire in a warehouse. There is usually no time to ask someone else what to do. Firefighters must be able to use their skills in new ways at any moment.

Professional fire fighting is teamwork. Firefighters spend a lot of time together. They eat together. They depend on one another as they battle the flames. They save one another's lives. Naturally, they come to have special feelings for one another. They become as close as a family. A firehouse is like a home.

Firefighters save lives and property. One thing is certain: the work they do is important. Firefighters have many chances to be heroes. They are often rewarded with medals for bravery. But most firefighters don't need medals as a reward for good work. They don't save lives to get a pat on the back. Saving a life is reward enough even if no one else knows you've done it. There are not many jobs where you can say to yourself at the end of a day, "Without me, that child would be dead."

SUITING UP FOR BATTLING BLAZES

Fire fighting is a lot safer if you're dressed for it. The perfect clothing would protect firefighters completely from heat, burns, injury, smoke, and poisonous gases, and still leave them free to move around to do their work.

The kind of suit most firefighters wear isn't perfect, but it has worked well enough to be used for many years. The leather helmet has a wide brim that keeps falling cinders from landing on the face or neck and lets water run off without getting inside the coat. It also acts as a hard hat to protect the head from injury due to falling objects. A rubber coat keeps out water and flame. The rubber boots have steel in the toe and heel to prevent foot injury. They can be pulled up to the hips to keep out water. A mask for breathing air is used to protect against smoke. Air is carried in tanks strapped on the back.

Ordinary fire fighting clothes are all right for ordinary fires. They are not good protection from very hot fires or in situations where you have to get close to flames. In fact, many fire departments are thinking of changing to more modern suits. A special fire fighting suit has been invented for pulling people out of burning aircraft. Perhaps some of the features of this suit will be built into suits for city firefighters.

This suit was tested in public not long ago. A man wearing the new supersuit for firefighters walked into an oven where the temperature was 1200°F. (Wood burns at 800°F.) He carried an armload of wood, a wicker chair, and a steak. After two minutes he came out of the oven, cool as an iceman. The wood was ablaze, the chair was destroyed, and the steak was well-done. To see the supersuit that gives the firefighter cool style, please turn the page. . . .

Mask (see below) seals
nose and throat off
from outside air.

Outside surface of suit is shiny aluminum that reflects
heat. It must be kept clean to do its job.

Wool shirt and pants may be worn under
the suit. Wool insulates to
prevent heat from reaching
the skin.

Hood covers breathing
mask.

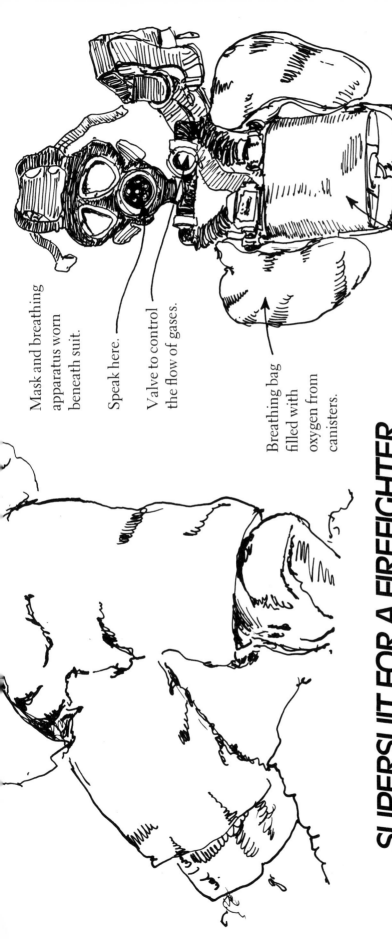

Mask and breathing apparatus worn beneath suit.

Speak here.

Valve to control the flow of gases.

Breathing bag filled with oxygen from canisters.

Canisters contain chemicals that produce oxygen gas. Carbon dioxide breathed out by firefighter is removed by chemicals.

SUPERSUIT FOR A FIREFIGHTER

The suit is a one-piece coverall. It's made of cotton and asbestos. Asbestos is a mineral that absorbs a great deal of heat without getting hot. There is growing evidence that asbestos fibers can cause severe lung problems. Unfortunately, science has not yet come up with a safer substitute that absorbs heat as well. So firefighters risk their health to save lives in special cases when they must get close to flames.

SEA SHANTY

"I love the sea because it has drowned me,"
    Said the sailor with the coral nose.
"I love the sea because it has fed me,"
    Said the lobster with grasping claws.

"Liquid I lived and liquid die,"
    Said the sailor with the coral nose.
"Give us this day our daily dead,"
    Said the lobster with grasping claws.
                         Clifford Dyment

3 *Going Under the Sea*

Billions of years ago life began in the sea. The earliest kinds of living things were very small and simple. Through the ages there were changes. Some living things became plants, and some became animals. Larger and more complicated forms of life developed. There came to be many different kinds of living things. Some stayed in the sea. Others came to live above water at the bottom of another kind of sea—a sea of air.

You are a distant relative of the first animals to come out of the sea. You are an even more distant relative of many animals that live in the sea today. The sea is no longer your home. Dive underwater and you know it. Within a minute or two you must come to the surface to fill your lungs with air. It's this need for air that has kept people above the surface of the sea for thousands of years. But it hasn't stopped us from wondering what's going on deep below.

It also hasn't stopped us from going down for a quick look. There have always been divers who have learned to exhale as they headed for the bottom. They've gone as deep as 145 feet. (That's as far below the surface as a fourteen-story building is above.) Within three or four minutes they are back at the surface. This kind of diving is

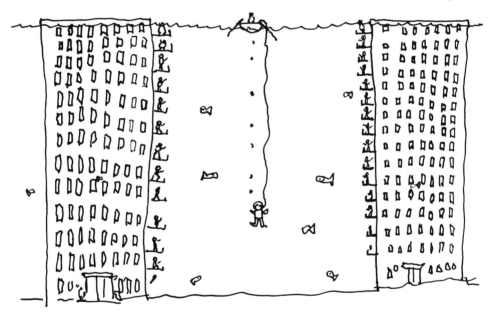

like eating only one piece of popcorn. Oh, to have a good long visit with the world under the sea! Many have died trying to make this dream come true.

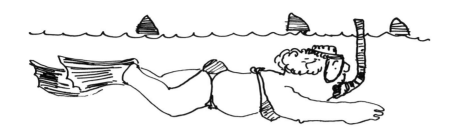

ABOUT AIR, LIFE, AND THE SEA

The answer seemed so simple. You need air to stay alive. There is no air underwater. Clearly, all you needed to do was take a supply of air when you went under. You could take air in a container. Or you could breathe through a tube that reached the surface.

There's nothing quite like trying out an idea to see how it works. It's true that you can keep your head underwater a long time by breathing through a tube to the surface. That's what snorkeling is. But you can't go very far from the surface, maybe only a few feet down. Certainly not far enough to get a good look at the ocean depths.

Here's the reason. When you are underwater, every part of your body is being pressed on by water above you. The deeper you go, the heavier the weight of the water pressing on you. If you go thirty-three feet beneath the surface (about three stories down), there are about 15 pounds of water pressing on each square inch of your body. This kind of pressure doesn't bother your arms and legs. But it

matters to your lungs. When you add up all the square inches on your chest, the weight of water is at least 150 pounds. It's like trying to breathe with your father sitting on your chest. Breathing muscles are just not strong enough to lift such a weight and let you fill your lungs.

The way to get around this problem is to make the air you breathe press against the *inside* of your lungs with the same force as water pressing against the *outside* of your chest.

The diving bell was designed to do this. On the surface the bell is full of air. A diver gets under the bell and stays in it as she or he dives. As long as the bell is held upright, air will not escape. (To see how this works, turn an empty glass upside down and push it straight down in a basin of water.) Water pushes against the air in the bell with the same force as it presses against the diver. Of course, in the process, the air is squeezed into a smaller space. There is a point where water pressure squeezes the air so much that there is no room for a diver's head. Divers just never purposely take a bell down deep enough for this to happen.

Diving bells were the best thing around for thousands of years. But they did have their problems. It was almost impossible for a diver in a bell to do much work or to walk around on the ocean floor. And every once in a while a bell tipped. Water rushed in, chasing away the air. On the surface there were bubbles signaling possible death under the sea.

Then, in the last century, a diving suit was invented. One of the most important parts of this suit is the air pump on the deck of a ship above the diver. Air is pumped into the helmet of the diving suit through a hose. The pressure of the air depends on the water pressure where the diver is. Divers one hundred feet down breathe air that presses with a force of about fifty pounds on each square inch of their lungs. At two hundred feet down, the air pressure is about one hundred pounds on each square inch.

Pressurized air is also pumped inside the suit. This is to make an air space over the chest so a diver can make the motions needed for breathing. Even at high pressure, air can be squeezed to take up less space, but water can't be squeezed much at all. When a diver breathes in, the chest gets larger, making the air space slightly smaller. Without an air space the crush of the water would be too great to allow the diver to draw breath, even with the help of an air pump.

If, for some reason, the pump fails or the hose or suit springs a leak, the crush of the sea takes over. Air in the suit rushes out of the hole, and the weight of the water squeezes the diver like a tube of toothpaste. On the surface, deckhands see a rush of bubbles, the sign of diver's squeeze, that almost always means gruesome death below.

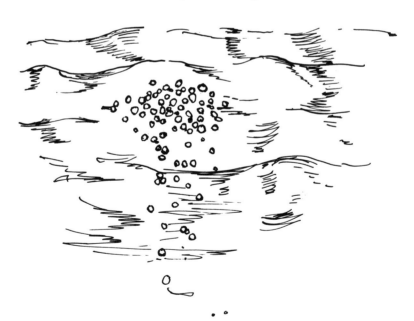

THE DANGERS OF THICK AIR

Air pumped to divers at high pressures is thicker than the air you are breathing now. One difference this makes is to the way your voice sounds. Pressurized air makes a voice sound much higher than normal. It also proved to have a few unhappy surprises for divers.

Air is a mixture of gases. You need only one gas of this mixture, oxygen, to stay alive. Only one part in every five parts of air is oxygen. Most of the rest of air is made up of another gas called nitrogen. When you breathe in, both gases enter your lungs. Oxygen is absorbed into your bloodstream. Nitrogen passes out of your lungs when you breathe out, and it doesn't enter your body unless it's under pressure.

Imagine going on a dive in a helmeted or "hard-hat" diving suit. As you stand on the deck, air comes through the hose at ordinary air pressure, like that of the air you're breathing now. You jump into the sea and start for the bottom. As you go down, water pressure gets higher. The pump sending you air keeps up with the changing water pressure. You don't feel any different because the pressure is the same on both the inside and outside of your lungs.

Within a minute or so you reach the bottom, two hundred feet below the surface. You feel fine, so you get busy doing the job you came down to do. After a while you begin feeling even better. You might start singing. Your voice sounds so funny in the thick air inside your helmet that you start laughing. You might even start dancing. If someone saw you, they might think you were drunk.

The truth is, you *are* drunk. You are good and high on nitrogen. Breathing too much nitrogen under pressure is like drinking too much wine. Divers have been known to fall asleep, forget where they are, or do foolish things. The bottom of the sea is no place to lose touch with reality. Getting drunk on nitrogen has been known to cost divers their lives.

Divers call a nitrogen high "rapture of the deep." They learn the warning signs of its fatal charms. They know when it's time to start the journey back to the surface.

Divers discovered that nitrogen is at its worst on the trip back up. While divers are on the bottom, nitrogen passes through their lungs and dissolves through their bodies. It goes everywhere, into blood, muscles, nerves, and skin. But more nitrogen goes into joints, such as shoulders, elbows, and knees, than any other parts of the body.

Dissolved nitrogen does no harm as long as it stays dissolved. High pressure keeps it that way. Things get rough as pressure lets up.

When pressure on a dissolved gas is suddenly lowered, there is a striking result—bubbles. You see this when you open a bottle of soda. Carbon dioxide is forced under pressure into flavored water in the process of making soda. Each bottle is sealed, keeping the pressure high. When you open a bottle, the pressure quickly drops. Bubbles form and rush to the top.

The same thing happens in a diver's body if the trip to the surface is too quick. Instead of carbon dioxide fizz, tiny bubbles of nitrogen form. Divers call these bubbles "black froth." Bubbles which form in blood vessels can cut off the supply of blood to different parts of the body. Bubbles can block nerves, making movement impossible. Since much of the nitrogen is in the joints, bubbles usually form there first. The diver will twist and turn to relieve the pain—a pain for which there are no words. For this reason the condition caused by black froth is called "the bends."

A diver doesn't have to get the bends. The trick is to get nitrogen to pass out of the body without forming bubbles. This happens if a diver returns *slowly* to the surface. How slowly depends on how deep and how long the dive was. About two hours are needed for the trip up after a diver spends a half hour at two hundred feet.

Divers can't safely go much below two hundred feet on pressurized air. On deeper dives, divers breathe a mixture of oxygen and helium, a very light gas used to blow up balloons. Helium won't cause rapture of the deep at high pressures.

Even with helium, few hard-hat dives are made to depths greater than three hundred feet. Bottom time is so short and the time up is so long on such deep dives that they are seldom worth making.

Despite its limits, hard-hat diving gives people useful time in many underwater places. It has been used for most dives for over a hundred years. Divers have learned to live with the ever-present dangers because going under the sea has paid off.

THE OLD HARD-HAT DIVING SUIT

Most underwater work is still done in a suit like this.

Rubberized cloth in one piece.

Helmet made of copper covered with tin.

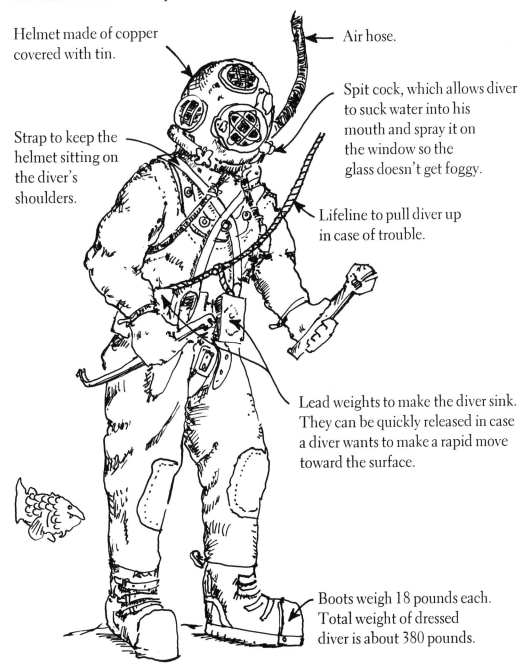

Air hose.

Spit cock, which allows diver to suck water into his mouth and spray it on the window so the glass doesn't get foggy.

Strap to keep the helmet sitting on the diver's shoulders.

Lifeline to pull diver up in case of trouble.

Lead weights to make the diver sink. They can be quickly released in case a diver wants to make a rapid move toward the surface.

Boots weigh 18 pounds each. Total weight of dressed diver is about 380 pounds.

REWARDS OF THE DEEP

There is beauty and mystery under the sea. Animals there often come in strange and wonderful shapes. Plants hide schools of flashing fish. The sea has been an inspiration to artists. Great music and poetry have been written about it. Sailors and fishermen have told countless stories of its power and glory.

But beauty and wonder have not been the only rewards for divers. The payoff for diving has been wealth. People have dived for oysters on the ocean floor. Oyster shells are valued for their smooth shiny insides called mother-of-pearl. Every once in a while there is a pearl in an oyster shell which brings in extra money, sometimes a large amount. Divers also have gone down to explore sunken ships, hoping to find valuable cargo. Most of the time the treasures that are supposed to be on board haven't been found. But there have been a few wrecks that paid off in gold and jewels. This was enough to keep treasure hunters diving for hundreds of years.

Today divers still go after sunken treasure. But other rewards have become more important. We must find new sources of fuel and new supplies of minerals to keep modern life going. The natural wealth of the land will be used up someday. One place left to look for these resources is underwater. Treasure hunters on the ocean floor these days are more likely to be looking for oil than for pirate gold.

People earn their living working underwater. Divers go down to lay pipes that will carry oil from tankers to shore. They build foundations for bridges and oil rigs. Divers harvest seaweed that is dried and fed to cattle. Divers are always needed to inspect and repair underwater structures.

Most hard-hat diving has been done by professionals. But in the 1960s scuba diving became popular, opening the undersea world to anyone who is interested. A scuba diver carries one or two tanks of air on his or her back. Air

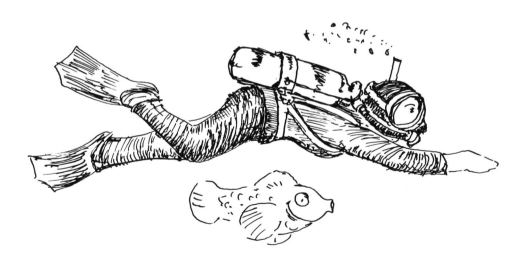

pressure is controlled by a special regulator as it is breathed. As in hard-hat diving, air pressure must be the same as water pressure. Scuba divers don't need an air hose or lifeline attaching them to the surface. They can move more freely than hard-hat divers. Nor do scuba divers need a boat with an air pump. This cuts the cost of diving. Scuba diving is so much fun that thousands are discovering the wonders of shallow waters near the shore. Deeper dives in scuba gear and in hard-hat suits are still made mostly by experts.

Diving for wealth, work, and fun has not taken us very far down into the ocean. Most diving is done over an underwater shelf off the coasts of continents. A continental shelf can extend hundreds of miles into the sea and reach a depth of six hundred feet before it drops off. The vast ocean floor is far below, at an average depth of thirteen thousand feet (2½ miles). It has flat plains, and mountains, and some very deep valleys. The deepest goes down

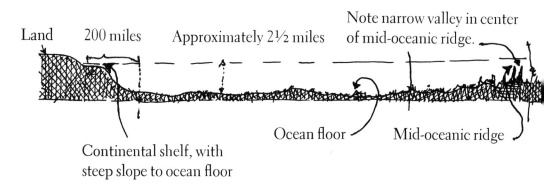

Cross section of ocean basin.

almost 7 miles. There the crushing pressure is more than two tons on each square inch!

No diver has ever walked about at these great depths. The few people who have gone down thousands of feet below the surface have been in tiny, specially built submarines. One man who was there said, "Below seven thousand feet there was no sun, no moon, no stars, only night and mystery." In the darkness he saw strange fish that had lights, like fireflies, as part of their bodies. This glimpse of "inner space" has made us want to see more.

The truth is, we know next to nothing about the sea. But we have learned enough to know that the greatest rewards for diving are yet to come. The Navy has projects that will lead to people spending weeks and months living and working a few hundred feet underwater. There are also projects to help us go deeper. Supersuits for deep dives are in the works. Turn the page to see the latest fashions for future undersea explorers. . . .

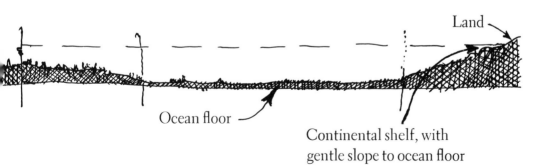

Ocean floor

Land

Continental shelf, with gentle slope to ocean floor

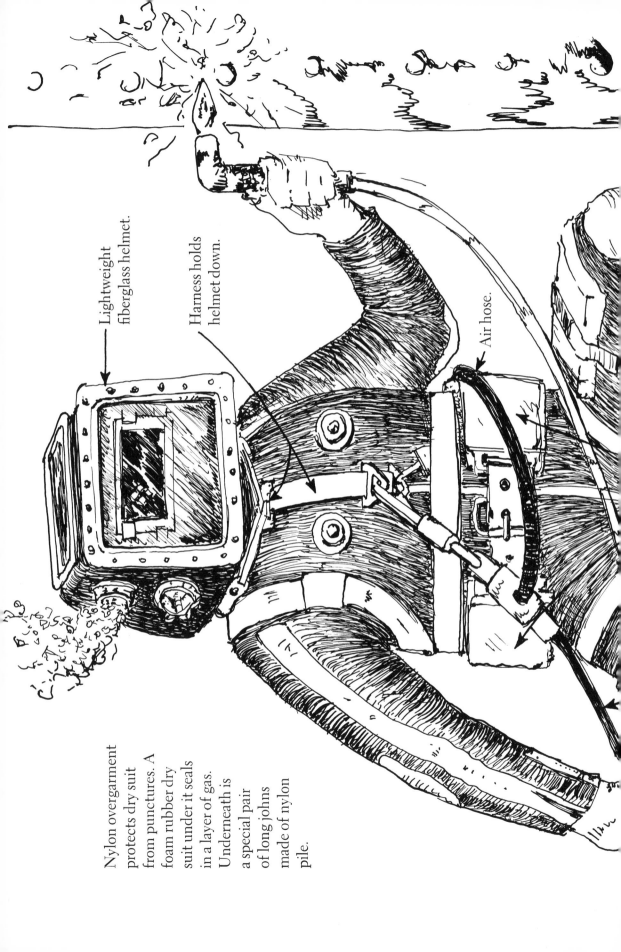

Lightweight
fiberglass helmet.

Harness holds
helmet down.

Air hose.

Nylon overgarment
protects dry suit
from punctures. A
foam rubber dry
suit under it seals
in a layer of gas.
Underneath is
a special pair
of long johns
made of nylon
pile.

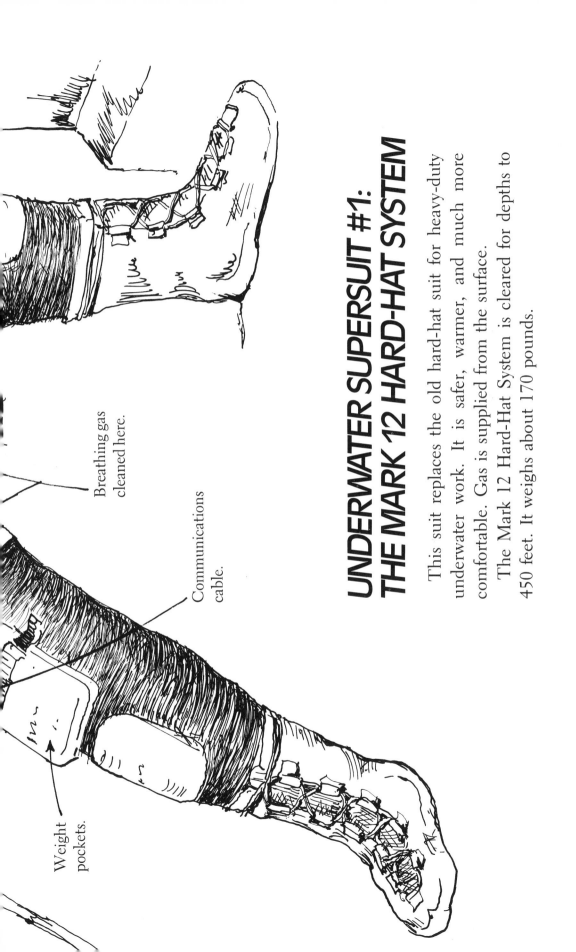

Breathing gas cleaned here.

Communications cable.

Weight pockets.

UNDERWATER SUPERSUIT #1: THE MARK 12 HARD-HAT SYSTEM

This suit replaces the old hard-hat suit for heavy-duty underwater work. It is safer, warmer, and much more comfortable. Gas is supplied from the surface.

The Mark 12 Hard-Hat System is cleared for depths to 450 feet. It weighs about 170 pounds.

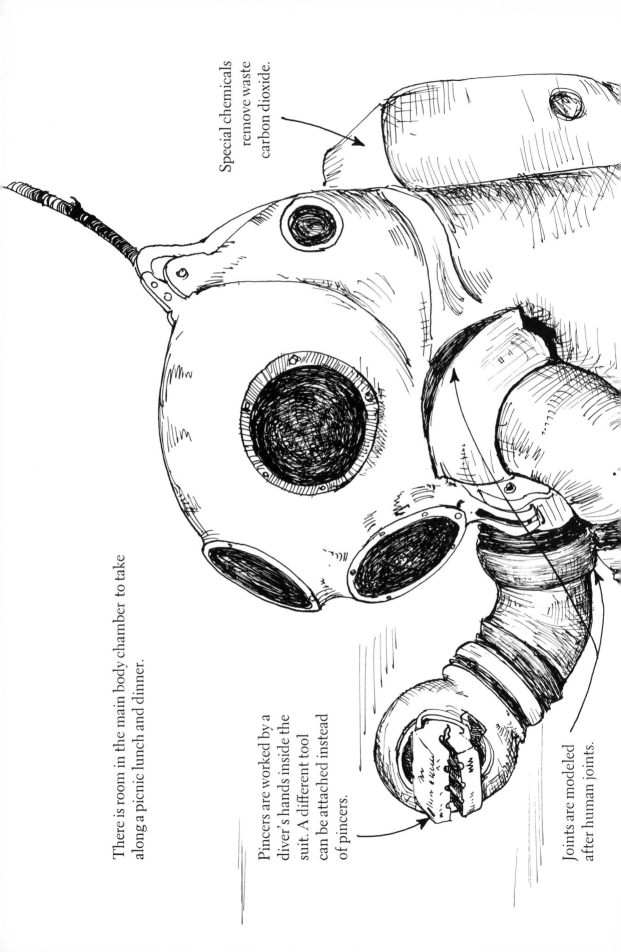

Special chemicals remove waste carbon dioxide.

There is room in the main body chamber to take along a picnic lunch and dinner.

Pincers are worked by a diver's hands inside the suit. A different tool can be attached instead of pincers.

Joints are modeled after human joints.

Lead weights to be released when a diver wants to surface.

The trip up from two hundred feet takes only two minutes.

UNDERWATER SUPERSUIT #2: JIM, THE ARMORED DIVER OF THE FUTURE

This metal diving suit is really a submarine shaped like a person. It is built to withstand pressures at depths of two thousand feet.

Air is breathed at ordinary pressure. It's supplied by a life support system that is taken along. There are none of the dangers of high-pressure nitrogen.

The suit weighs 910 pounds when empty. In water a person doesn't notice it is that heavy.

A diver in this suit can walk up a ladder or pick up pennies from the ocean floor.

HOW TO TELL THE TOP OF A HILL

The top of a hill
Is not until
The bottom is below.
And you have to stop
When you reach the top
For there's no more UP to go.

To make it plain
Let me explain:
The one *most* reason why
You have to stop
When you reach the top—is:
The next step up is sky.

John Ciardi

4 *Going Where the Air Is Thin*

A strange thing happens when you take off in an airplane, or ride a high-speed elevator in a skyscraper, or even when you drive up a steep hill. As you go higher and higher, you get an uncomfortable feeling—clogged ears. You open your mouth in a wide yawn. Pop, your left ear clears. Another yawn and the right one opens. Clogged ears are one sign that air in high places is not quite the same as air on the ground.

Air is like a sea that completely covers the earth. Just as the ocean presses down on divers, our sea of air, the earth's atmosphere, puts pressure on us. Air seems to be such flimsy stuff that it's hard to believe it presses with a force of almost fifteen pounds on each square inch of your body. Usually you don't feel air pressure. Air inside your body, in your lungs and head, pushes back with the same force as outside air pressing against you.

Air gets thinner as you move higher. Air pressure gets lower, just as water pressure eases up on a diver heading for the surface. When you travel up in a high-speed elevator, outside pressure drops slightly. Inside pressure, in your head, remains what it was on the ground. You feel this difference in pressure in your ears.

Some people leave the comfort of good, thick air behind. They travel miles upward, where the view of earth is wide. For them it is a heady thrill to be where the air is thin.

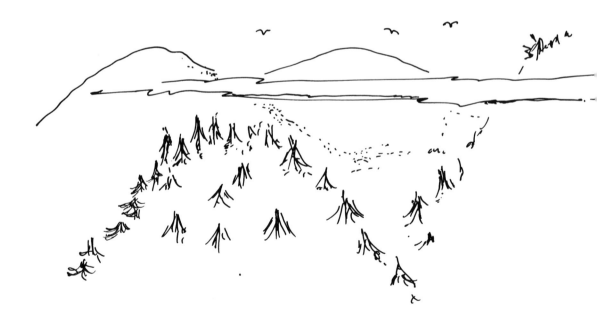

CLIMBING TO HIGH GROUND

The bottom line of our atmosphere is sea level. There are some inland valleys below this line, but most land rises above it. You don't have to live at sea level to be comfortable. You can get used to living in much higher places.

Thousands live in the highest city in the world, La Paz, Bolivia. It's in the Andes Mountains, 11,966 feet (more than two miles) above sea level. Citizens of La Paz don't notice its thin air. But you would if you went to visit. On the long ride up the mountain you would notice pressure changes in your ears. The insides of your ears are connected to your nose and throat. When you yawn, you let out extra air, making inside pressure the same as outside pressure. This unclogs your ears, making pressure changes easier to handle.

Mountain sickness is another story. Thin air means less oxygen as well as lower pressure. Your body is used to getting as much oxygen as it needs with each breath you draw. If you suddenly find yourself in thin air, your body gets slightly oxygen-starved. It's enough to make you sick!

A mild case of mountain sickness may last only one or two miserable days. You have a pounding headache. You are dizzy. You breathe faster and harder than usual. It's as if you've been running when you've only been walking. You feel sleepy. Everything might look blurred. You might also feel as if you have to throw up.

Your amazing body starts working to change this state of things. Blood has the job of carrying oxygen to all parts of your body. Millions of tiny red bodies called red blood cells hook up with oxygen brought in by your lungs. At high altitudes each breath brings in less oxygen than usual. So your body starts making extra red cells. (It's like a trucking business where the load each truck can carry becomes smaller. So you bring in more trucks.) When you have enough red cells to supply you with as much oxygen as you need, mountain sickness disappears. When you return to the richer air of lower altitudes, the extra red cells disappear.

There are, of course, places on earth higher than La Paz. The highest is Mount Everest. It towers 29,028 feet (5½ miles) above the sea. The challenge is to reach the top on foot, no easy trick. Climbing Everest is a project that takes months and a team effort.

The base of Everest is quite high, more than three miles up. A climbing team hires many local people to help carry equipment and supplies to the base of the mountain. The weeks spent at this job give team members plenty of time to get over mountain sickness. Their bodies become better able to handle the even thinner air above them on the mountain.

Everest must be climbed in stages. Camps are set up along the way. Each camp is higher than the one below. Equipment and supplies are moved in backpacks from lower camps to higher ones. Team members work for weeks, making trip after trip up and down between camps. But it is not possible to carry up enough supplies for the whole team to reach the top. In the end perhaps only two climbers will reach the summit.

The mountain is not a friendly place. The temperature drops when the air gets thin. Mount Everest is always covered with ice and snow. Even under a hot sun, temperatures on the summit can reach 30°F below zero. No wonder some call Everest "the third pole."

Walking through snow isn't easy. It's even harder when you're wearing bulky clothing and have a heavy pack on your back. It's harder still when you're chopping steps up an icy mountainside. At heights where you're starved for oxygen, every move takes a major effort.

Above twenty-three thousand feet the extra red cells your body made at the base don't seem to be much help. The air is too thin to supply extra cells with oxygen. Climbing and living in thin air and bitter cold take willpower. You breathe about eight times for each step up. There is pain in your ears and throat. You hear your heart pounding. Everything, even your thoughts, seems to be in slow motion. This is especially dangerous where you must be quick-witted to keep from making a false step.

At camp you don't feel like eating. You have a hard time sleeping. You're almost always thirsty. Yet you must move on. Too much time spent at these great heights can do permanent damage to your brain.

Mountain climbers have found there is only one way to have a chance of reaching the summit of Everest. They must take along oxygen. They must spend as short a time as possible above twenty-three thousand feet. They must wear clothing designed to protect them against the cold, the bright snow, and the thin air. People who climb Everest hardly look human. . . .

SUPERSUIT FOR THE HIGHEST GROUND OF ALL

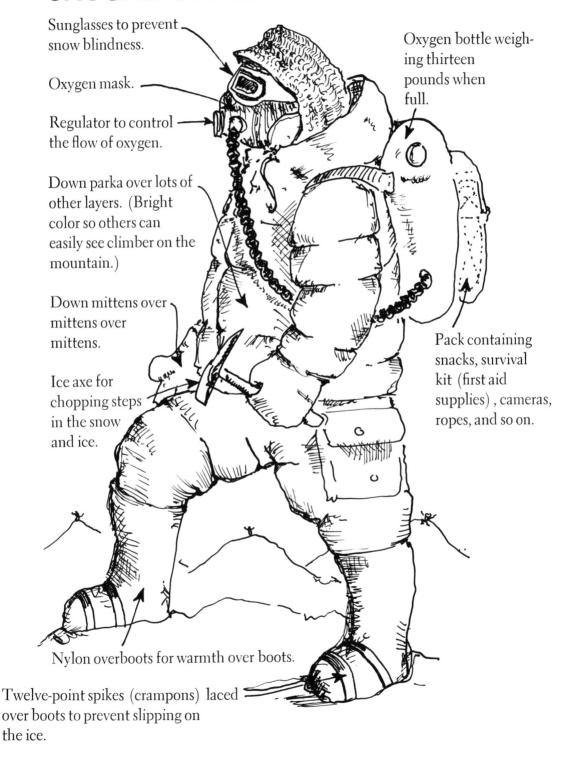

Sunglasses to prevent snow blindness.

Oxygen mask.

Regulator to control the flow of oxygen.

Down parka over lots of other layers. (Bright color so others can easily see climber on the mountain.)

Down mittens over mittens over mittens.

Ice axe for chopping steps in the snow and ice.

Oxygen bottle weighing thirteen pounds when full.

Pack containing snacks, survival kit (first aid supplies) , cameras, ropes, and so on.

Nylon overboots for warmth over boots.

Twelve-point spikes (crampons) laced over boots to prevent slipping on the ice.

BALLOONING

Mountain climbing is a long, tough way to reach high places. It's much easier and quicker to take a ride straight up in a balloon.

Ballooning is the oldest kind of air travel. The first people to ride a balloon took off about two hundred years ago. Their blue and gold balloon was filled with hot air. It rose only a few hundred feet and stayed up only twenty-five minutes. But this first ride showed others a new way to explore the upper parts of our atmosphere.

No one knew what to expect from air thousands of feet above sea level. So in 1862, two Englishmen decided to take a ride to find out. Their names were Glaisher and Coxwell. And they almost didn't live to tell the tale.

On the afternoon of September 5, Glaisher and Coxwell stepped into the open basket of their balloon. The sky was overcast. The air was a mild 59°F. Their spirits were good. Soon they would be higher than anyone else had ever been.

The purpose of their trip was scientific. They were to collect air samples as they rose. They were to measure temperature. They even took along six pigeons to see how they flew from different altitudes. Glaisher and Coxwell didn't know their trip would answer another question: How high can people go before dying?

The balloon contained a gas that was lighter than air. Sandbags kept the balloon from rising too fast. Coxwell dumped sand overboard to make the balloon rise. Glaisher was busy reading his instruments.

They broke through the clouds at eleven thousand feet. The sky was dark blue and the tops of the clouds below them were like a field of white cotton. The temperature was dropping as they rose. Coxwell began feeling the lack of oxygen. It was getting harder and harder to dump sand overboard. But he didn't pay any attention to this warning. One problem caused by oxygen starvation is that you have a false sense of well-being.

When they reached twenty-five thousand feet, Glaisher's vision started to go. He could hardly see his instruments. He had an even harder time just moving. He later wrote about how he felt when he reached twenty-nine thousand feet—well above the height at which Everest climbers start using oxygen. "I struggled and shook my body, but could not move my arms. Getting my head upright for an instant only, it fell on my right shoulder." As the balloon continued to rise, Glaisher went blind and then passed out.

Luckily, Coxwell, who couldn't move his arms either, was able to use his teeth to open the valve that let gas out of the balloon. As gas escaped, the balloon began moving down. Glaisher came to when they reached thicker air. His sight also returned. They had been about thirty-five thousand feet or 6½ miles up without using oxygen. Both men returned to earth safely and lived to a ripe old age.

Today we know just how lucky Coxwell and Glaisher were. Not everyone who breathes such thin air survives. Pilots are told to start using oxygen at ten thousand feet. Modern jets usually travel higher than thirty-five thousand feet, but passengers don't need to breathe oxygen because cabins are filled with pressurized air. Over each seat is an oxygen mask in case cabin pressure fails. Before every flight the cabin attendant must, by law, show passengers how to use the oxygen mask.

As for balloons, we've gone higher and higher—just over twenty miles above the earth. Here a balloon bobs up and down like a cork on the surface of the sea of air.

Hanging underneath is a pressurized cabin. Safe inside is a modern-day balloonist.

BAILING OUT

It was quite clear from the beginning of air travel that there had to be an emergency backup system. People needed a safe way to reach the ground if an aircraft was crippled during a flight. So the parachute was invented a few years after the first balloon ride.

Parachutes are a success story. Without them, objects falling from airplanes hit the ground at speeds above 125 miles an hour. A parachute slows an object down so it lands at a speed you can live with—16 miles an hour. Parachutes are used to land people and supplies in out-of-the-way places. They are used for the fast-growing sport of sky diving. But the main use for parachutes is to escape from planes that are going to crash.

When you bail out at twenty thousand feet, thin air isn't much of a problem. Within seconds you reach fifteen thousand feet. Your parachute opens automatically, and you slowly drift through thick air to safety.

There are military planes that fly in very thin air, sixty thousand feet and above. If you bail out at these great heights, it takes minutes to fall to fifteen thousand feet. Minutes in this very thin air can spell death. Cabin air pressure in high altitude aircraft is about ten pounds on each square inch of your body. Outside air pressure is about one pound. The drop in pressure is quite a shock.

All of a sudden there is almost no force pressing down on your outside. Gas inside your body swells to take up more space. Air escapes from your head and lungs through your mouth. But gas in your stomach has no way out. It puffs up like a balloon pressing against your lungs, making it hard to breathe.

There's not much up here to breathe anyway. Within fifteen seconds you pass out from lack of oxygen. And higher up it's even worse. Above seventy-three thousand feet (about eleven miles) the temperature is 55°F below zero. Lack of oxygen gives you only five seconds before passing out. Lack of pressure causes a problem that is even more certain to kill you—your blood boils without getting hot. Bailing out at these great heights can mean death long before you reach the ground.

Yet, the record parachute jump was made from a balloon over one hundred thousand feet high. The man who made the jump spent several minutes passing through the death zone of thin air before reaching the safety of fifteen thousand feet. He survived because he was dressed for the occasion.

A supersuit for very thin air must be able to do several jobs. It must be able to supply oxygen for breathing. It must put pressure over the lungs. This is to help push air out of the lungs when breathing. The suit must also put pressure over the rest of the body to prevent blood from doing a cold boil and to keep it flowing evenly through the body. The suit must be strong enough to resist the tremendous blast of wind that hits a flyer when bailing out. It also must protect the person against low temperatures. On top of all this, a suit for thin air should be fairly comfortable. Sometimes cabin pressure fails, but the aircraft can still fly. The crew may have to spend hours bringing the aircraft safely home. They need protection against low pressures and temperatures that invade the cockpit. But they must also be able to move and do their jobs. The supersuit that does all this is worn by all crew members flying above sixty thousand feet. To see the fashion for high flyers, please turn the page. . . .

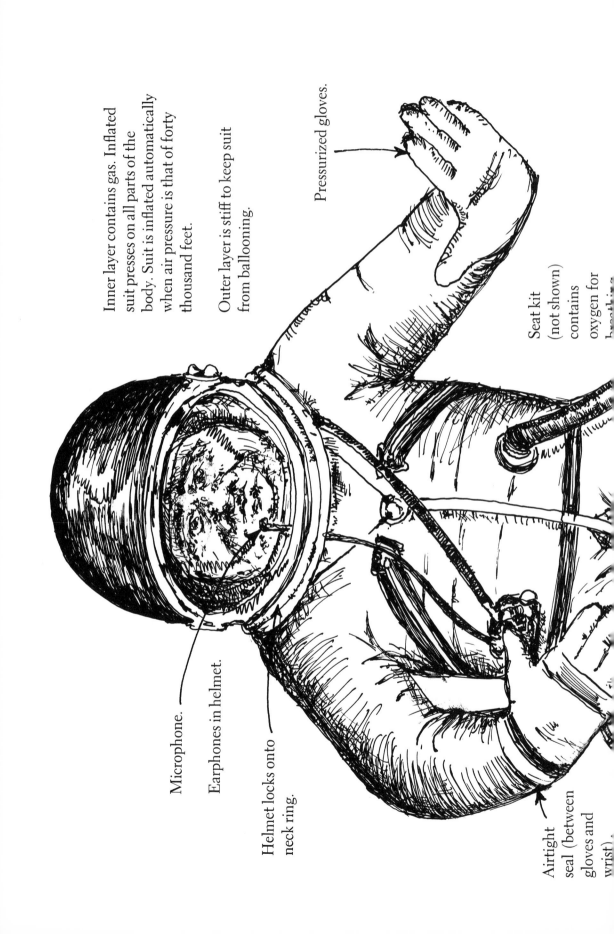

Inner layer contains gas. Inflated suit presses on all parts of the body. Suit is inflated automatically when air pressure is that of forty thousand feet.

Outer layer is stiff to keep suit from ballooning.

Pressurized gloves.

Seat kit (not shown) contains oxygen for breathing.

Microphone.

Earphones in helmet.

Helmet locks onto neck ring.

Airtight seal (between gloves and wrist).

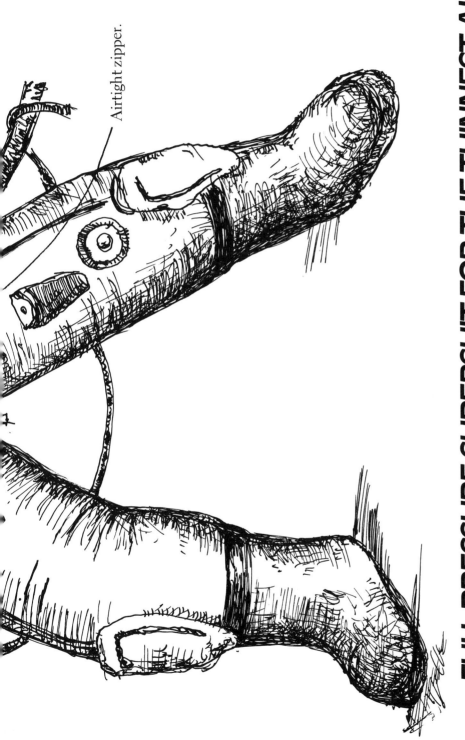

Airtight zipper.

FULL PRESSURE SUPERSUIT FOR THE THINNEST AIR

This suit is built to protect against wind and against wet and dry cold.

SWEEPING THE SKY

There was an old woman tossed up in a basket,
Ninety times as high as the moon;
And where she was going, I couldn't but ask it,
For in her hand she carried a broom.

"Old woman, old woman, old woman," quoth I,
"Whither, O whither, O whither so high?"
"To sweep the cobwebs off the sky!"
"Shall I go with you?" "Aye, by-and-by."

Author unknown

5 Going to Near and Outer Space

Since the beginning of history the human race has been wondering about the sky. It wasn't hard to think up questions: Where does the sun get its heat? What is the moon made of? How did the universe begin, and how will it end? Myth and fable gave easy answers to these questions and more. True answers were hard to come by. Even today there are great gaps in what we know for sure.

In the past we couldn't leave earth on our search for truth. The message from the heavens was clear: Look but don't touch.

It's amazing how much we've learned just by looking.

Except for a few rocks (meteorites) that accidentally land on earth, the only thing that comes here from space is light. Reading light from space is an astronomer's job.

The size and brightness of stars tell how far away and how large they are. Colors of stars and sun are clues to what they are made of and where they get their energy. The motions of stars reveal the motion of the earth. The shape of light reflected off planets tells us where they are.

Astronomers have special instruments to collect and examine light from space. In addition to telescopes they use special cameras and sensitive films to show up small changes that might not be seen any other way. They can even collect light we can't see, radio and cosmic waves that are clues to the birth and death of stars.

When all this information is put together, it's very clear that space is a most unfriendly place. There is nothing, absolutely nothing, out there to keep people alive. The distances between other planets and earth are so great that space travel would take chunks of a lifetime, even for a one-way visit. Most of the closer stars are more than a lifetime away.

But the dream of space travel is built into us. And now, after taking our first steps outside earth, we are not about to give up our dream.

HARDWARE TO GET US THERE

There was no way we could set one foot in space unless we could escape the earth. Earth has a grip (called gravity) on all things on or near its surface. To escape this pull an object must travel twenty-five thousand miles an hour. It takes a lot of power to get a five-pound ball going that fast. Building rockets to give that kind of power to a spacecraft weighing several tons was one of the great engineering feats of this century.

Instead of one rocket, a team of three rockets launched the Apollo moon trips. First the biggest and most powerful rocket lifted the spacecraft and the other rockets off the ground. As it sped from earth's surface, it built up a force four times the strength of gravity. (This made the crew feel four times as heavy as they feel on the surface of the earth. They could hardly move.)

When its job was finished, the big rocket dropped off and fell back into the ocean. A second, smaller rocket was now exposed. It fired to increase the speed of a now much lighter spacecraft-rocket. Then the second rocket dropped off, and a third pushed the spacecraft into orbit at a speed of eighteen thousand miles per hour. Spacecraft can "park" in earth orbit. They circle the earth every hour and a half without ever needing to use their engines. (Earth orbit is called "near space.") To leave earth orbit for the moon, astronauts fired the third engine again to build up to the escape speed of twenty-five thousand miles per hour.

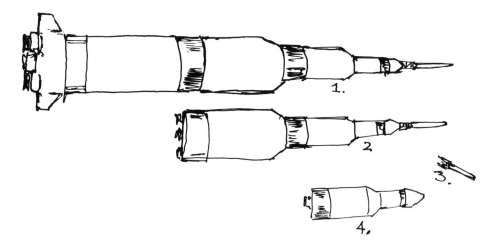

Apollo command spacecraft on moon trips were packed with everything each crew member might need for eight days. They also contained equipment for experiments to be performed on the moon. Attached to the command ship was another spacecraft that actually carried two of the crew to the surface of the moon and back to the command ship. While the moon was being explored, the third astronaut orbited the moon, no doubt enjoying the extra room.

Being cramped during an eight-day trip is one thing. Living and working in space for months at a time is another. Future space trips beyond the moon will take months, even years. If we are ever to make such journeys, we must know if astronauts can stand space—and each other—for long periods of time.

Skylab was a project designed to begin answering this question. Skylab was much larger and more comfortable than the spacecraft used for moon trips. It had a galley with a food table, sleeping compartments, and a shower. (Outside earth's gravitational field, water sort of hangs in space, so a space shower is more like a bag. Droplets float around inside the bag. Rubbing with a soapy washcloth still works, however.) It had exercise machines to keep the crew from getting flabby. And it had a workroom for collecting information and setting up experiments. Skylab never escaped earth but parked in earth orbit while three separate crews took turns on board. They used Apollo spacecraft to make the round trip between earth and Skylab. Skylab crews set new records for time spent living and working in space.

The next spacecraft to come off the drawing board will be the space shuttle. It will take off like a rocket, orbit like a spacecraft, and land like a jet. It will be used to carry people and supplies back and forth from earth orbit. Instead of being used only once, as were launching rockets, the space shuttle will be used for hundreds of trips, just like an airplane. It will be so comfortable that anyone in good health will be able to ride in it. You won't need the special training given to astronauts.

After the space shuttle there are plans for a space tug. It will be used to launch satellites and spacecraft from earth orbit to outer space. If we go to Mars in 1985, the space shuttle and space tug will probably play their parts in the beginning and end of the journey.

DOWN-TO-EARTH REWARDS FROM SPACE

Back in the 1950s, Russia surprised the world by launching the first unmanned satellite. At that time America hadn't put much effort into exploring space. Many Americans felt that, if Russia was sending up satellites, America should develop its space program too. And so America started the manned Apollo project and shot for the moon.

Now America and Russia have decided there is more to be gained from cooperating in space than from keeping up separate programs. The next people in space may be part of a joint American and Soviet effort.

The U.S.A.'s manned space program had a high price tag. It would have been a lot cheaper to stick to small unmanned space probes and satellites. The giant booster rockets and spacecraft used for only one manned trip cost Americans billions of dollars.

Many people complained during the years of construction, "Why spend all that money to put people on the moon?" People were saying the same kind of thing to Queen Isabella of Spain before Columbus set off on uncharted seas and came to discover America. The fact is, you can't give a really good answer to that question until after you make the trip. Going into the unknown has paid off. It paid off for Columbus, and space is starting to pay off for us.

One thing is certain: space is a great place for sun and star gazers. Our view of the heavens from earth is somewhat fuzzy because of the atmosphere. Beyond our sea of air the view is clear. Telescopes in space have been turned on the sun. Among the fruits of these observations may be new ways to capture the sun's energy for use on earth—a hope in times of energy shortage. Meanwhile, astronomers are busy sorting and sifting piles of other information collected from space telescopes.

Space is also a good place for earth watching. Skylab

crews spotted pollution and plant disease. They measured the size of crops. They searched for schools of fish in the oceans and for new places to drill for oil. It seems clear that information from space can help us use earth's resources to greater advantage

The manned space projects showed us something about ourselves. Never before in history have so many people worked as a team to turn a dream into reality. There was no such word as "impossible." As problems came up, new materials and products were designed to solve them. Some of these materials and products are now turning up in everyday life.

A tragic accident during a training session led to the development of new antifire materials. The breathing gas used in Apollo command ships was pure oxygen—a fire hazard if ever there was one. One day it happened. A flash fire took the lives of three astronauts. The spacecraft was redesigned, using fireproof paint. Unlike most paint, which burns easily (ask any firefighter), fireproof paint swells up in a fire to protect underlying structures. In addition, space suits were redesigned. Now they are made from Beta Cloth, a glass fabric. Beta Cloth doesn't burn and is now being used in some fire fighting suits.

Spinoffs from space are proving useful in many different areas. Electronic devices from space systems are used in collars to keep track of wild animals. Special metals used to cover rockets are being used for capping and drilling teeth. Speed-measuring inventions for spaceships are being used by police to detect speeding drivers. Little by little people are finding earthly use for small pieces of space technology. One of these days it may all add up to a big payoff.

WHY STEP OUTSIDE?

Space is very much like the outer layer of our atmosphere, only worse. There is simply nothing there to breathe. There is absolutely no pressure—space is an almost perfect vacuum—blood does a cold boil if any part of the body is exposed.

Surface temperature in sunlight can go as high as 250°F. (Water boils at 212°F.) And in the shadows it can be 250°F below zero. Here and there you might find tiny pieces of rock (micrometeoroids) speeding along like bullets. Unhappily, they also act like bullets if they strike soft flesh. And there is no air to protect against deadly ultraviolet and cosmic rays that act like an overdose of X-rays.

Space travelers could, of course, remain safe and comfortable inside a spacecraft. But right from the beginning it was clear that space explorers would not stay behind glass and only look.

If we were going to the moon, we were going to get our hands on it. We were going to bring home pieces of our nearest neighbor. Scientists on earth were waiting with an army of instruments. At long last no more guesswork from afar! This was the chance of all lifetimes to discover what the moon was *really* made of. And here was a chance to set up experiments on the moon that could send information back to earth long after astronauts had left.

Besides, stepping outside might be a backup measure in case there were problems during a mission. There's no telling when someone with a screwdriver, able to float in space, might be very useful. The lives of the astronauts could be endangered because something that could be reached only from outside the ship needed repair.

As it happens, an outside repair job saved the Skylab mission. Panels that collect energy from the sun were not working properly. Had it not been for a spacewalk to repair the panels early in the first mission, there's a good chance Skylab would have been a failure. During a Skylab mission jet-powered backpacks were tested. They will someday turn spacewalks into spacezooms as astronauts zip quickly from one spot to another.

Astronauts on spacewalks have been busy with other tasks. The usual job has been to change film in cameras attached to the outside of spacecrafts. (These cameras take wide angle pictures not possible from inside. The pictures are used to make maps of the sun, earth, and moon.) Film has to be removed before returning to earth. Otherwise it will be destroyed in the fireball that develops when the spacecraft hits the atmosphere.

Stepping into space is built into the future of space exploration. Astronauts will leave spaceships to do rescue work and to repair and maintain the many unmanned satellites orbiting earth (satellites that let us watch television from Europe and predict tomorrow's weather, to name two). Astronauts will step outside to transfer people and cargo from one spacecraft to another. And someday there's a good chance that spaceships to other parts of the universe will be put together in earth orbit by teams of orbiting construction workers.

Naturally, no one would dare step outside a spacecraft unless properly clothed. The well-dressed astronaut wears nothing less than a space suit—the supersuit that stands for space adventure.

A space suit must do many of the jobs other supersuits do. It must protect against very cold and very hot temperatures. It must supply life-supporting, breathable gas. Like full pressure suits, it must keep blood from boiling and collecting in different parts of the body. This posed a problem for space suit designers. Pressure suits are extremely stiff. Pressure comes from blowing up the suit with a gas. It is almost impossible to bend an inflated suit. (Try bending a balloon to see how stiff it can be.) You can't pick up

moon rocks in that kind of suit. Moveable joints were a victory for space suit designers.

A radio system must be built into a space suit, for space

is silent. Sound travels through matter, such as air or water. There can be no sound where there is no matter. Astronauts face to face cannot hear each other even if they yell. Only radio and lip reading make communication possible.

The space suits that have been worn so far are custommade for individual astronauts. They fit perfectly. Future space suits will come in standard sizes to be worn by the average space traveler. But it's not likely that styles will change much from the space suit on the next page. . . .

SPACE SUIT: THE LAST WORD IN SUPERSUITS

Total weight of suit and PLSS: 180 pounds on earth. (In space, it weighs nothing; on the moon it weighs about 30 pounds.) Price tag: $130,000.

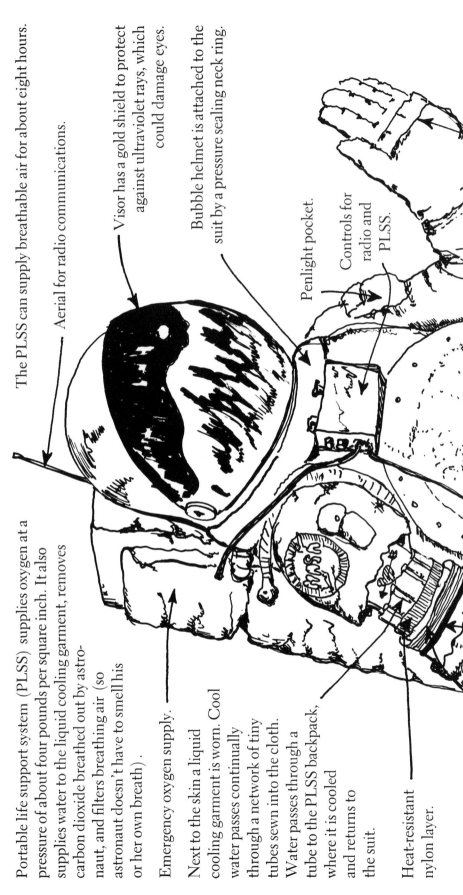

The PLSS can supply breathable air for about eight hours.

Aerial for radio communications.

Visor has a gold shield to protect against ultraviolet rays, which could damage eyes.

Bubble helmet is attached to the suit by a pressure sealing neck ring.

Penlight pocket.

Controls for radio and PLSS.

Portable life support system (PLSS) supplies oxygen at a pressure of about four pounds per square inch. It also supplies water to the liquid cooling garment, removes carbon dioxide breathed out by astronaut, and filters breathing air (so astronaut doesn't have to smell his or her own breath).

Emergency oxygen supply.

Next to the skin a liquid cooling garment is worn. Cool water passes continually through a network of tiny tubes sewn into the cloth. Water passes through a tube to the PLSS backpack, where it is cooled and returns to the suit.

Heat-resistant nylon layer.

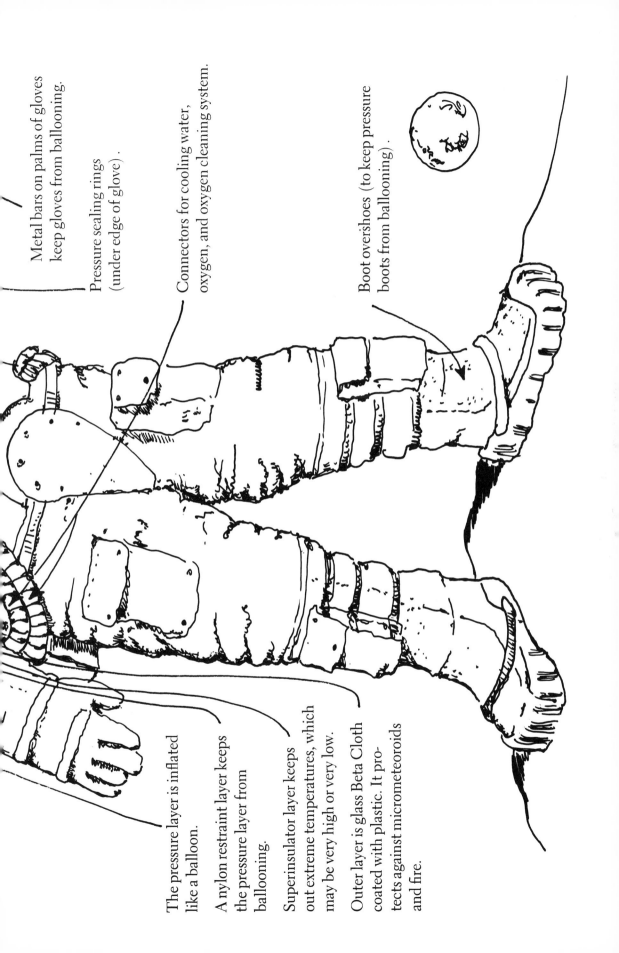

Metal bars on palms of gloves keep gloves from ballooning.

Pressure sealing rings (under edge of glove).

Connectors for cooling water, oxygen, and oxygen cleaning system.

Boot overshoes (to keep pressure boots from ballooning).

The pressure layer is inflated like a balloon.

A nylon restraint layer keeps the pressure layer from ballooning.

Superinsulator layer keeps out extreme temperatures, which may be very high or very low.

Outer layer is glass Beta Cloth coated with plastic. It protects against micrometeoroids and fire.

Index

Page numbers in italics refer to illustrations.

About the Author

Vicki Cobb received her early education at the Little Red School-house and attended the University of Wisconsin on a Ford Foundation Early Admissions Scholarship. She earned a bachelor's degree from Barnard College and a master's degree in secondary school science education from Columbia University Teachers College.

Ms. Cobb has taught general science and physical science at Rye High School, Rye, New York, and at the Manhattan Day School in New York City. She is the author of several books for young people.

About the Illustrator

Peter Lippman lives in New York City where he has studied at the Art Students' League and Columbia University School of Fine Arts. He has won many awards for his illustrations and paintings and his work is often featured in *The New York Times* and other periodicals. He has illustrated several books for children.

Also by Vicki Cobb

Science Experiments You Can Eat

How the Doctor Knows You're Fine

Arts and Crafts You Can Eat

DISCARD